JUST BEFORE CHRISTMAS

Children's Stories to Read Aloud

Illustrated by NATASHA SIMKHOVITCH
Edited by THERESA RICE ENGELS

Partridge Press

Special thanks to Ethel Boyle for cover paintings and line
art recreated from the original illustrations; Ann Blattner
for cover design; and Sarah Koper for design assistance.
Color reproductions by Carter Color, Inc. Typography,
North Star Press of St. Cloud, Inc. Printed in the United
States of America by Walsworth Publishing Company,
Marceline, Missouri.

© 1994, Partridge Press
ISBN: 0-9621085-8-8

Published by *PARTRIDGE PRESS*
P.O. Box 364
St. Cloud, MN 56302
612-253-1145
Stephen E. Engels, Publisher

CONTENTS

THE CHRISTMAS CUCKOO
Frances Browne

Once upon a time there stood in the midst of a bleak moor, in the North Country, a certain village. All its inhabitants were poor, for their fields were barren, and they had little trade; but the poorest of them all were two brothers called Scrub and Spare, who followed the cobbler's craft. Their hut was built of clay and wattles. The door was low and always open, for there was no window. The roof did not entirely keep out the rain and the only thing comfortable was a wide fireplace, for which the brothers could never find wood enough to make sufficient fire. There they worked in most brotherly friendship, though with little encouragement.

On one unlucky day a new cobbler arrived in the village. He had lived in the capital city of the kingdom and, by his own account, cobbled for the queen and the princesses. His awls were sharp; his lasts were new; he set up his stall in a neat cottage with two windows. The villagers soon found out that one patch of his would outwear two of the brothers'. In short, all the mending left Scrub and Spare, and went to the new cobbler.

The season had been wet and cold, their barley did not ripen well, and the cabbages never half-closed in the garden. So the brothers were poor that winter, and when Christmas came they had nothing to feast on but a barley loaf and a piece of rusty bacon. Worse than that, the snow was very deep and they could get no firewood.

Their hut stood at the end of the village; beyond it spread the bleak moor, now all white and silent. But that moor had once been a forest; great roots of old trees were still to be found in it, loosened from the soil and laid bare by the winds and rains. One of these, a rough, gnarled log, lay hard by their door, the half of it above the snow, and Spare said to his brother:

"Shall we sit here cold on Christmas while the great root lies yonder? Let us chop it up for fire wood, the work will make us warm."

"No," said Scrub, "It's not right to chop wood on Christmas; besides, that root is too hard to be broken with any hatchet."

"Hard or not, we must have a fire," replied Spare. "Come, brother, help me in with it. Poor as we are there is nobody in the village will have such a yule log as ours."

Scrub liked a little grandeur, and, in hopes of having a fine yule log, both brothers strained and strove with all their might till, between pulling and pushing, the great old root was safe on the hearth, and beginning to crackle and blaze with the red embers.

In high glee the cobblers sat down to their bread and bacon. The door was shut, for there was nothing but cold moonlight and snow outside; but the hut, strewn with fir boughs and ornamented with holly, looked cheerful as the ruddy blaze flared up and rejoiced their hearts.

Then suddenly from out the blazing root they heard: "Cuckoo! cuckoo!" as plain as ever the spring bird's voice came over the moor on a May morning.

What is that?" said Scrub, terribly frightened; "it is something bad!"

"Maybe not," said Spare.

And out of the deep hole at the side of the root, which the fire had not reached, flew a large, gray cuckoo, and lit on the table before them. Much as the cobblers had been surprised, they were still more so when it said:

"Good gentlemen, what season is this?"

"It's Christmas," said Spare.

"Then a merry Christmas to you!" said the cuckoo. "I went to sleep in the hollow of that old root one evening last summer, and never woke till the heat of your fire made me think it was summer again. But now since you have burned my lodging, let me stay in your hut till the spring comes round—I only want a hole to sleep in, and when I go on my travels next summer be assured I will bring you some present for your trouble."

"Stay and welcome," said Spare, while Scrub sat wondering if it were something bad or not.

"I'll make you a good warm hole in the thatch," said Spare. "But you must be hungry after that long sleep—here is a slice of barley bread. Come help us to keep Christmas!"

The cuckoo ate up the slice, drank water from a brown jug, and flew into a snug hole which Spare scooped for it in the thatch of the hut.

Scrub said he was afraid it wouldn't be lucky; but as it slept on and the days passed he forgot his fears.

So the snow melted, the heavy rains came, the cold grew less, the days lengthened, and one sunny morning the brothers were awakened by the cuckoo shouting its own cry to let them know the spring had come.

"Now I'm going on my travels," said the bird, "over the world to tell men of the spring. There is no country where trees bud, or flowers bloom, that I will not cry in before the year goes round. Give me another slice of barley bread to help me on my journey, and tell me what present I shall bring you at the twelvemonth's end."

Scrub would have been angry with his brother for cutting so large a slice, their store of barley being low, but his mind was occupied with what present it would be most prudent to ask for.

"There are two trees hard by the well that lies at the world's end," said the cuckoo; "one of them is called the golden tree, for its leaves are all of beaten gold. Every winter they fall into the well with a sound like scattered coin, and I know not what becomes of them. As for the other, it is always green like a laurel. Some call it the wise, and some the merry, tree. Its leaves never fall, but they that get one of them keep a blithe heart in spite of all misfortunes, and can make themselves as merry in a hut as in a palace."

"Good master cuckoo, bring me a leaf off that tree!" cried Spare.

"Now, brother, don't be a fool!" said Scrub; "think of the leaves of beaten gold! Dear master cuckoo, bring me one of them!"

Before another word could be spoken the cuckoo had flown out of the open door, and was shouting its spring cry over moor and meadow.

The brothers were poorer than ever that year. Nobody would send them a single shoe to mend, and Scrub and Spare would have left the village but for their barley field and their cabbage garden. They sowed their barley, planted their cabbage, and, now that their trade was gone, worked in the rich villagers' fields to make out a scanty living.

So the seasons came and passed; spring, summer, harvest, and winter followed each other as they have done from the beginning. At the end of the latter Scrub and Spare had grown so poor and ragged that their old neighbors forgot to invite them to wedding feasts or merrymakings, and the brothers thought the cuckoo had forgotten them, too, when at daybreak on the first of April they heard a hard beak knocking at their door, and a voice crying:

"Cuckoo! cuckoo! Let me in with my presents!"

Spare ran to open the door, and in came the cuckoo, carrying in one side of its bill a golden leaf larger than that of any tree in the North Country, and in the other side of its bill one like that of the common laurel, only it had a fresher green.

"Here," it said, giving the gold to Scrub and the green to Spare. "It is a long carriage from the world's end. Give me a slice of barley bread, for I must tell the North Country that the spring has come."

Scrub did not grudge the thickness of that slice, though it was cut from their last loaf. So much gold had never been in the cobbler's hands before, and he could not help exulting over his brother.

"See the wisdom of my choice," he said, holding up the large leaf of gold. "As for yours, as good might be plucked from any hedge; I wonder a sensible bird would carry the like so far."

"Good master cobbler," cried the cuckoo, finishing its slice, "your conclusions are more hasty than courteous. If your brother is disappointed this time, I go on the same journey every year, and for your hospitable entertainment will think it no trouble to bring each of you whichever leaf you desire."

"Darling cuckoo," cried Scrub, "bring me a golden one."

And Spare, looking up from the green leaf on which he gazed as though it were a crown jewel, said:

"Be sure to bring me one from the merry tree."

And away flew the cuckoo.

"This is the feast of All Fools, and it ought to be your birthday," said Scrub. "Did ever man fling away such an opportunity of getting rich? Much good your merry leaves will do in the midst of rags and poverty!"

But Spare laughed at him, and answered with quaint old proverbs concerning the cares that come with gold, till Scrub, at length getting angry, vowed his brother was not fit to live with a respectable man; and taking his lasts, his awls, and his golden leaf, he left the wattle hut, and went to tell the villagers.

They were astonished at the folly of Spare, and charmed with Scrub's good sense, particularly when he showed them the golden leaf, and told that the cuckoo would bring him one every spring.

The new cobbler immediately took him into partnership; the greatest people sent him their shoes to mend. Fairweather, a beautiful village maiden, smiled graciously upon him; and in the course of that summer they were married, with a grand wedding feast, at which the whole village danced except Spare, who was not invited, because the bride could not bear his low-mindedness, and his brother thought him a disgrace to the family.

As for Scrub he established himself with Fairweather in a cottage close by that of the new cobbler, and quite as fine. There he mended shoes to everybody's satisfaction, had a scarlet coat and a fat goose for dinner on holidays. Fairweather, too, had a crimson gown, and fine blue ribbons; but neither she nor Scrub was content, for to buy this grandeur the golden leaf had to be broken and parted with piece by piece, so the last morsel was gone before the cuckoo came with another.

Spare lived on in the old hut, and worked in the cabbage garden. (Scrub had got the barley field because he was the elder.) Every day his coat grew more ragged, and the hut more weather-beaten; but people remarked that he never looked sad or sour. And the wonder was that, from the time any one began to keep his company, he or she grew kinder, happier, and more content.

Every first of April the cuckoo came tapping at their doors with the golden leaf for Scrub, and the green for Spare. Fairweather would have entertained it nobly with wheaten bread and honey, for she had some notion of persuading it to bring two golden leaves instead of one; but the cuckoo flew away to eat barley bread with Spare, saying it was not fit company for fine people, and liked the old hut where it slept so snugly from Christmas till spring.

Scrub spent the golden leaves, and remained always discontented; and Spare kept the merry ones.

I do not know how many years passed in this manner, when a certain great lord, who owned that village, came to the neighborhood. His castle stood on the moor. It was ancient and strong, with high towers and a deep moat. All the country as far as one could see from the highest turret belonged to its lord; but he had not been there for twenty years, and would not have come then, only he was melancholy. And there he lived in a very bad temper. The servants said nothing would please him, and the villagers put on their worst clothes lest he should raise their rents.

But one day in the harvest time His Lordship chanced to meet Spare gathering water cresses at a meadow stream, and fell into talk with the cobbler. How it was nobody could tell, but from that hour the great lord cast away his melancholy. He forgot all his woes, and went about with a noble train, hunting, fishing, and making merry in his hall, where all travelers were entertained, and all the poor were welcome.

This strange story spread through the North Country, and great company came to the cobbler's hut—rich men who had lost their friends, beauties who had grown old, wits who had gone out of fashion—all came to talk with Spare, and, whatever their troubles had been, all went home merry.

The rich gave him presents; the poor gave him thanks. Spare's coat ceased to be ragged, he had bacon with his cabbage, and the villagers began to think there was some sense in him.

By this time his fame had reached the capital city, and even the court. There were a great many discontented people there; and the king had lately fallen into ill humor because a neighboring princess, with seven islands for her dowry, would not marry his eldest son.

So a royal messenger was sent to Spare, with a velvet mantle, a diamond ring, and a command that he should repair to court immediately.

"Tomorrow is the first of April," said Spare, "and I will go with you two hours after sunrise."

4

The messenger lodged all night at the castle, and the cuckoo came at sunrise with the merry leaf.

"Court is a fine place," it said, when the cobbler told it he was going, "but I cannot come there; they would lay snares and catch me; so be careful of the leaves I have brought you, and give me a farewell slice of barley bread."

Spare was sorry to part with the cuckoo, little as he had of its company, but he gave it a slice which would have broken Scrub's heart in former times, it was so thick and large. And having sewed up the leaves in the lining of his leather doublet, he set out with the messenger on his way to court.

His coming caused great surprise there. Everybody wondered what the king could see in such a common-looking man; but scarcely had His Majesty conversed with him half an hour, when the princess and her seven islands were forgotten and orders given that a feast for all comers should be spread in the banquet hall.

The princes of the blood, the great lords and ladies, the ministers of state after that discoursed with Spare, and the more they talked the lighter grew their hearts, so that such changes had never been seen at court.

The lords forgot their spites and the ladies their envies, the princes and ministers made friends among themselves, and the judges showed no favor.

As for Spare, he had a chamber assigned him in the palace, and a seat at the king's table. One sent him rich robes, and another costly jewels; but in the midst of all his grandeur he still wore the leather doublet, and continued to live at the king's court, happy and honored, and making all others merry and content.

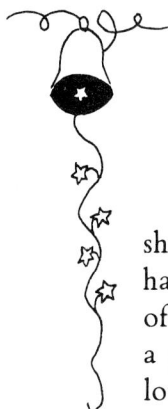

AN EARLY ENGLISH CHRISTMAS BLESSING

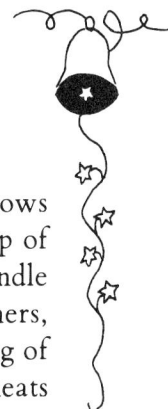

Whosoever on the night of the nativity of the young Lord Jesus in the great snows shall fare forth bearing a succulent bone for the lost and lamenting hound, a whisp of hay for the shivering horse, a cloak of warm raiment for the stranded wayfarer, a bundle of fagots for the twittering crone, a flagon of red wine for him whose marrow withers, a garland of bright berries for one who has worn chains, a dish of crumbs with a song of love for all huddled birds who thought that song was dead, and divers lush sweetmeats for such babes' faces as peer from lonely windows—

To him shall be proffered and returned gifts of such astonishment as will rival the hues of the peacock and the harmonies of heaven. Though he live to a great age when man goes stooping and querulous because of the nothing that is left in him, yet shall he walk upright and remember as one whose heart shines like a great star in his breast.

JEST 'FORE CHRISTMAS

Father calls me William, sister calls me Will,
Mother calls me Willie, but the fellers call me Bill!
Mighty glad I ain't a girl—ruther be a boy,
Without them sashes, curls, an' things that's worn by Fauntleroy!
Love to chawnk green apples an' go swimmin' in the lake—
Hate to take the castor-ile they give for belly-ache!
'Most all the time, the whole year round, there ain't no flies on me,
But jest 'fore Christmas I'm good as I kin be!

Got a yeller dog named Sport, sick him on the cat;
First thing she knows she doesn't know where she is at!
Got a clipper sled, an' when us kids goes out to slide,
'Long comes the grocery cart, an' we all hook a ride!
But sometimes when the grocery man is worried an' cross,
He reaches at us with his whip, an' larrups up his hoss,
An' then I laff an' holler, "Oh, ye never teched *me*!"
But jest 'fore Christmas I'm good as I kin be!

Gran'ma says she hopes that when I git to be a man,
I'll be a missionarer like her oldest brother, Dan,
As was et up by the cannibuls that lives in Ceylon's Isle,
Where every prospeck pleases, an' only man is vile!
But gran'ma she has never been to see a Wild West show,
Nor read the *Life of Daniel Boone,* or else I guess she'd know
That Buff'lo Bill and cow-boys is good enough for me!
Except' jest 'fore Christmas, when I'm good as I kin be!

And when old Sport he hangs around, so solemn-like an' still,
His eyes they keep a-sayin': "What's the matter, little Bill?"
The old cat sneaks down off her perch an' wonders what's become
Of them two enemies of hern that used to make things hum!
But I am so perlite an' tend so earnestly to biz.
That mother says to father: "How improved our Willie is!"
But father, havin' been a boy hisself, suspicions me
When jest 'fore Christmas, I'm as good as I kin be!

For Christmas, with its lots an' lots of candies, cakes an' toys,
Was made, they say, for proper kids an' not for naughty boys;
So wash yer face an' bresh yer hair, an' mind yer p's and q's,
An' don't bust out yer pantaloons, an' don't wear out yer shoes;
Say "Yessum" to the ladies, an' "Yessur" to the men,
An' when they's company, don't pass yer plate for pie again;
But, thinking of the things yer'd like to see upon that tree,
Jest 'fore Christmas be as good as yer kin be!

Eugene Field

7

THE SMALL ONE OF BETHLEHEM
Charles Tazewell

The late December sun that dances on the winter snow up north sprawls indolently at ease in the thick warm dust of El Camino del Norte, Old Mexico.

It was once upon a Christmas time that a padre, his robe gray from the Norte's dust, and his cheeks two ripe holly berries from the heat, sought out the cool dripping shade of a pepper tree and dropped off to sleep—a habit and privilege of the very old.

Then suddenly his midday siesta was shattered by a shrill, indignant voice. His heavy eyelids opened to see a small boy standing with bare brown legs wide apart in the middle of the road and bitterly addressing a small, discouraged and most disreputable donkey.

"A donkey! A *donkey,* you call yourself, Estupido! A fine animal with a stout leg on each corner—with a splendid and serviceable tail to shoo away the flies and two handsome ears stuck on the front to point the way you are going! Asi! And of what use do you make of all this excellent equipment with which the good God has blessed you? Nothing! Nothing but *nothing!*"

The padre sighed and closed his eyes, but the boy's voice continued, riding the heat waves that rose in giddy spirals from the dust of El Camino del Norte.

"You a donkey? You are a disgrace to all the donkeys of all Mexico! Of all the world! Of all the universe!"

"Pablo!" The padre abandoned all hope of midday dreaming. "Pablo, my son!"

"Si? Oh, . . . Oh, buenas dias, Padre! I—I did not know you were there!"

"That I can believe. Whatever is the trouble? What has the poor beast done that you should be so angry?

The boy hung his head and his toes drew embarrassed doodle marks in the dust.

"The donkey has done nothing, Padre."

"Then why do you scold him?"

"Because nothing is all he ever wants to do! Here it is—but two days until Christmas, when a load of wood could be sold in the village to buy gifts for my mother and a candle for the church! But does that matter to this donkey? No, not at all!"

The padre laughed and the boy's donkey raised one questioning ear.

"Well—a donkey's a donkey, Pablo. One is like all the others."

"But *why?* Why, of all beasts must a donkey be so—so *stubborn?*"

"Stubborn?" The padre's face became serious. "Oh no, Pablo, that's wrong! A donkey isn't stubborn."

"But, Padre—!"

"Oh, I know, I know! Everyone *says* they are. People curse them and belabor their small backs with sticks and call them lazy and stupid. They do that because they don't know the truth about little donkeys."

The boy's eyes studied his diminutive animal seeking some hidden and incredible mystery.

"The truth, Padre?"

"Yes! It's really not stubbornness but pride that makes all small donkeys so—well so aloof. No sun, wind, storm, pain or adversity can ever touch them. That's because their pride is a shield against anything that men or the elements can offer."

"Pride?" The boy's eyes were scornful. "What has a donkey to be proud of?"

"Oh, a great deal, Pablo! Yes, indeed. Come, bring your little animal over here in the shade and I'll tell you all about it."

The boy gave a tug on the frayed and knotted rope and the donkey opened his eyes. Upon seeing that their probable destination was only a few steps away, and that a succulent yucca might be within easy nibbling range, he plodded docilely along behind the boy to the shelter of the pepper tree.

The padre turned his head and listened, and a smile illumined the intricate pattern of lines on his benevolent face.

"Listen, Pablo! Do you hear that? Only a small donkey can make that sound with his hoofs as he walks on the stones of the road. It's almost like music. Yes, yes, it's very like a song I once heard the chimes playing from the tower of the great cathedral one Christmas morning. . . . Sit down—sit down, my son."

"Si, Padre."

"Now, Pablo, as I said, people are all wrong about little donkeys. What people often mistake for laziness is pride—pride in a very great honor that came to one of them a long, long time ago. This honor was so final and complete that it lifted him and all his many, many descendants to an exalted place. Yes, a place that you and I and all the world might envy! And so, ever since that time, all small donkeys have been content to stand and drowse in the sun or shade, for he, alone, of all other animals—and of all men—has already fulfilled his destiny."

The boy puzzled for a moment over this baffling statement. "His destiny, Padre?"

"Yes, Pablo. You see, once upon a time, many miles and years from here, there lived a small donkey. He was fourteen unhappy years old, and he had worked hard and long for at least twice fourteen masters. He was battered and scarred, and his tail was naught but a piece of limp rope, unraveled down at the end. One of his ears stood straight up like a cactus plant, while the other ear hung down like a wilted cabbage leaf. Yes, and his off-hind leg had a decided limp."

"And what did they call this miserable donkey?"

"His name was Small One. His latest master was a woodcutter, who also owned four younger and therefore stronger donkeys."

"Was the woodcutter good to him?"

"His son was. It was the boy who saw to it that Small One always had dry straw for his bed and that the load of wood to be carried to the town wasn't too heavy for Small One's aging back."

"They were what we call amigos?"

"That's right. Amigos. Friends. Very good friends. Well, early one morning, in that season of the year when even the sun itself seems loath to rise and thrust shivering beam into the cold of the valleys, the woodcutter called his son to him and said,

"Son, I have an errand for you to do in the town."

"Yes, father? A load of wood?"

"No. No, I wish you to take the old donkey—the one you call Small One—to a shop just in-

side the town gates."

"Yes, father."

"I have already spoken to the man who owns the shop. He will give you one piece of silver in exchange for the animal."

"You mean—?" There was sudden alarm and fear in the boy's face. "You *don't* mean you're going to sell Small One!"

"Why not?" The father pretended not to see his son's distress and hurried on. "Why, even when carrying half the load of the other donkeys, his worn-out legs tremble and his sides heave like a bellows!"

"But he'll be as strong as the others soon!" The boy was all eagerness to defend any fault in his friend. "You wait and see! Just give him a few weeks!"

"An old donkey is of no use to anyone! One day soon he might drop dead on us up in the hills—a total loss. It's better to take the piece of silver now and say good riddance to the beast. You will start at once."

The boy, striving to hold back the hot tears, nodded his head. The father went on, trying to speak lightly as if it were a matter of little consequence.

"The shop where you will take the donkey is the second on the left as you pass through the town gates."

"The second on the left?" The sudden realization of the fate in store for Small One turned the boy's grief into horror. "But—but that's the tanner's!"

"And what of that?" The father spoke gruffly to cover his own discomfort. "The beast's hide is old, but it will make good leather."

"But he's been faithful! He's worked hard! He's done his best!" The boy's face was convulsed with misery and despair. "You can't sell him to the tanner to be killed!"

"Come, now, I'll have no tears!" The father hardened his heart and made his voice stern. "Shame on you—crying over a miserable donkey! Now, hurry—be off with you! If you start at once, you can be home before nightfall. And remember—take good care not to lose that piece of silver."

The father strode off to begin the day's work, and the boy picked up the old strap that was Small One's single earthly possession and placed it around the little donkey's neck. Then, following the wood path to the road, the small boy and the small donkey began their sorrowful journey to the town.

People along the way wondered why the boy was crying. They couldn't know that he was listening to Small One's hooves on the road—and the hooves seemed to beat out the words "Going to the tanner's . . . Going to the tanner's . . . Going to the tanner's."

And all along the miles, the boy tried to think of some way to save his friend. Suddenly, as they came in sight of the great town gates, he remembered there was a horse market in the Square. Yes, and if he could sell Small One to some new and kind master, the little donkey wouldn't be killed and yet his father would still receive his piece of silver!

It was high noon when the boy and Small One came to the horse market, a place filled with the shouts and loud voices of men and the acrid-sweet smell of leather and horse sweat. Tied to a long rail were all the animals to be sold—twenty sleek, beautiful mares and stallions, long of mane and tail, rubbed and brushed and combed until their coats glistened and shone in the sunlight like burnished copper or polished ebony. The auctioneer, a burly, red-faced man, stood on a platform and harangued the uplifted faces of the prospective buyers.

The boy, surprised at his own courage, lifted his hand and tugged on the auctioneer's robe.

"Please, sir—this small donkey's for sale!"

"Eh?" The auctioneer looked down over his cascade of fat chins. "Go away, boy, go away!"

"But he's a very fine donkey! He's not nearly as old as he looks—and this ear, the one that doesn't stand up straight as a donkey's should—that was the fault of a careless master! He's very strong and he eats very little!"

"This is a horse market, boy!" The auctioneer tried to shake off the hand that held tight to his robe. "I haven't time to waste on a miserable donkey!"

"But, please—please—wouldn't a small donkey take such a small time?"

The auctioneer burst into a mountainous roar of laughter that shook the platform.

"All right! All right, my boy—since you insist!" Then, lifting his voice, he addressed the crowd. "Gentlemen, your attention, please! This is indeed a day of days, for I have a wonderful bargain to offer you! Just feast your eyes on this strange object in front of my platform. What is it, do you ask? Well, the owner assures me that it is a donkey, but to my poor old eyes it has the appearance of an animated pile of shaking bones!" The auctioneer paused while the crowd laughed its approval of his statement. "Look closely, my friends, and you will observe how the moths have eaten at its hide! And the tail! Is it a tail? I believe it's only the stub of an old broom, worn out from sweeping the courtyard!" The market place echoed with shouts, howls and guffaws of the men. "A true and rare museum piece, my friends—moldly with age and loose in the joints!"

"He's not!" The boy's outraged voice rose over the din. "He's not like that at all!"

"Ah!" The auctioneer struck a pose of mock humility. "But it is not seemly to laugh, my friends, because—so his proud owner assures me—because this ancient ruin is distinguished enough to share a stall with the king's horses!"

"Don't say those things about him; it isn't true! The boy's voice was almost drowned out by the rolling waves of laughter. "Maybe he isn't so handsome as all your animals, but he's better!" He hugged the little donkey's head close to his breast and his angry tears fell on the rough, brown hairs of Small One's nose. "Yes—and he *is* fine enough to be in a king's stable—and maybe someday that's where you'll find him!"

"All right, all right, my boy!" The auctioneer was anxious to get on with the bidding while the crowd was in a good mood. "Take your precious donkey and move along; we've used up enough good time on you! Go on—hurry up!"

And so, with the auctioneer's fading voice in their ears, the boy and his donkey left the market place. The hours were slipping swiftly by, and before long he must start for home—and when he arrived there, he must have the piece of silver for his father.

Two small weary legs and four old ones began a dogged, despairing journey through the town. A frantic childish voice called to people as they hurried by on the streets. A trembling whisper spoke of a tremendous bargain at doors that were angrily closed with a shouted, "Be off with you!" No one in all the town desired to buy an old, tired donkey.

It was close to sundown when the boy and Small One returned to the town gates and stood outside the tanner's door. The boy's hand fondled the rough brown nose, caressed the drooping ear, and patted the worn coat for the last time. Then, just as he lifted the latch of the tanner's door, a voice spoke to him from the street. "My son!"

"Yes?" The boy turned hopefully. "Yes, sir?"

A bearded, poorly dressed man detached himself from the crowd that was moving toward the town gates.

"Tell me—are you the owner of this small donkey?"

"Yes, sir."

"I have a long journey to make and my wife is not well. I have a great need of a strong, gentle animal to carry her safely."

"Oh, Small One is very strong—and very trustworthy!"

The man looked from the donkey's old eyes to the two young ones. "Oh, yes—I can believe that. Would you be good enough to sell him to me?"

"Oh, yes, sir!" The boy's heart sang at the miracle. The price is but one piece of silver!" The man was looking at Small One's drooping ear. "Is that too much, Sir?"

"Too much?" The man smiled down at him. "No, indeed! Why, that's very reasonable for such a beautiful animal."

The boy was almost overcome by this unexpected appreciation of Small One.

"Well . . . Well, he's not really very beautiful . . . but he's good."

"One piece of silver, you said." The man took a torn leather pouch from his belt, a pouch that was so flat that its contents could be only a few coins. What is it you call him?"

"Small One." The boy watched the man's finger explore the bottom of the pouch. Suppose the man was only joking like the auctioneer? Suppose he didn't have one piece of silver?

"Ah, yes—Small One." The man held out a shining silver piece and dropped it in the boy's hand. "There you are, my son—and I promise you I'll be very kind to him. Come, now, Small One, we have to hurry. It's near to sundown, and the guards will be closing the town gates!"

The little donkey seemed puzzled at the tug of a strange hand on his strap, and then he started slowly but obediently off at the side of his new master.

The boy watched them disappear into the crowd, standing on tiptoe to catch a last glimpse of that one long ear that stood up straight as a donkey's should. His happiness at having saved Small One's life was now lost in the dreadful pain of losing him. Suddenly his legs started to run, carrying him through the crowd in swift pursuit. He overtook Small One and his new owner just a few steps from the great town gates.

"Please, sir—!" his breath had been left far behind at the tanner's door—"please, may I watch you through the gates? You see, Small One and I—!"

"Why, of course!" The man nodded his head in understanding. "You want to say good-by to your friend. You can do that while I see my wife safely on his back. Easy, now, Small One."

Standing in the shelter of the wall was a woman wrapped in the folds of a heavy traveling robe. As the man went to her side and took her arm to guide her, the boy whispered his last good-by.

"Good-by, Small One. You must be very faithful—and this isn't forever, you know. When I grow up—and earn many pieces of silver—I'll buy you back. Then you'll have a fine stable, and nothing to do but eat and sleep. . . . Won't that be wonderful, Small One?"

"All right, my son." The man's hand touched his shoulder. "We're ready to start."

The old donkey lifted his head at the pull on his strap, and bearing the woman on his work-worn back moved slowly and carefully toward the gates. Suddenly the voice of the guard called out a sharp command.

"Wait! One moment, traveler!"

"Yes?" The man's voice was patient. "Yes, soldier?"

"Your name?"

"My name is Joseph."

"And your wife?"

"They call her Mary."

"Your destination?"

The man looked toward the hills beyond the gate. "We journey to Bethlehem."

"Pass, traveler."

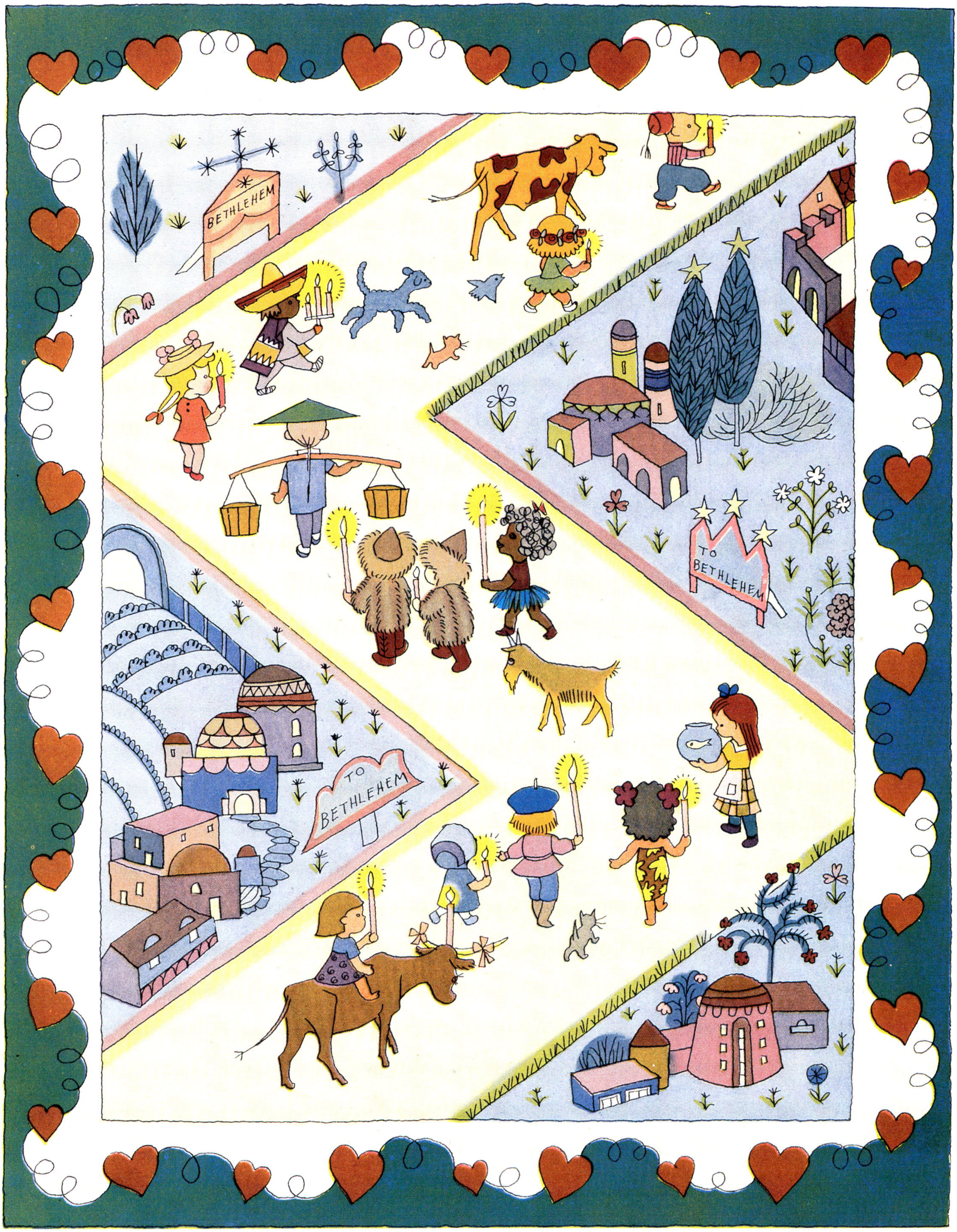

And so Joseph and Mary and Small One passed through the town gates, and the donkey's hooves rang sharply on the stones of the road—and the sound was very much like music. The boy called a last farewell to the gathering dusk.

"Good-by! . . . Good-by, Small One! . . . Be gentle and sure of foot . . . and carry her safe to Bethlehem!" . . .

The voice of the padre who sat in the cool shade of the pepper tree by El Camino del Norte, Old Mexico, was silent—his thoughts still far away on his story of a boy and a donkey in the long ago. The little donkey that had inspired the telling of the story, stood with his eyes closed and seemed asleep. Pablo, his young master, waited for a moment and then said, "And so, Padre?"

"And so, Pablo, the Small One traveled the weary miles to Bethlehem; there, in a stable, which became a King's stable, he saw a King born. A King of men—of centuries—of life—of death. Yes, and the Small One's tired old eyes saw the Wise Men and Shepherds who came to pay homage to his small Master and his dim old ears heard the voices of angels rejoicing and singing the very same notes that his own small hooves had sung out on the stones of the road. Then it came to pass that all those who had laughed at his ragged coat, and his limping gait, and his drooping ear, they all came to envy the Small One, for he had traveled the road to Bethlehem to become a part of a great miracle. . . . Lazy, did you say, Pablo? Ah, no, little donkeys are proud! You and I and everyone have far to travel, but long centuries ago they fulfilled their destiny. Yes, and that's why all small donkeys stand and dream—especially at Christmas time—dream of the Small One, the Small One of Bethlehem."

The padre, Pablo and the small donkey were quiet. A cool breath of air from the hills ventured down El Camino del Norte, foretelling that soon the long evening shadows would creep across the road from their hiding place among the tall yucca plants.

The air was sweet with sage and carried the sound of music. Was it the distant bells in the tower of the great cathedral, rehearsing their chimes for Christmas morning . . . or was it merely the sound of some small donkey's hooves as he plodded his way homeward?

They listened—the padre, the boy, his little donkey.

They listened—yes—but only the donkey really knew.

CHRISTMAS THROUGH A KNOTHOLE
Katharine Gibson

Old Hans, the best woodcarver in all Saxony, was thrown into prison just three weeks before Christmas. Again and again he had been told not to hunt in the Duke's own hunting grounds. Again and again his mouth would water for the taste of jugged hare, and to the Duke's lands he would go to set his snares. The jailer was kindly and, since Hans was old, he let him have a fire and some blocks to whittle on. But Hans was very unhappy. To be in jail on Christmas when all the village was celebrating!

Hans lived all alone. But he had a special friend. Her name was Gretchen; she was seven years old and had big gray eyes and long, smooth yellow hair in two pigtails. Gretchen had a little brother; he was as brown and ruddy as she was pink and white. He was as lively and full of mischief as she was bright and thoughtful.

"Oh, Max," Gretchen said to her little brother, "what shall we do? Poor Onkel Hans in jail and just for hunting rabbits. He always has his Christmas dinner with us, and now he won't have any—not a bite."

"And worse than that," said Max, "we won't get any toys." Each year Old Hans carved the most wonderful toys for them, sometimes whole villages with people and animals.

Max looked very cross and sulky and Gretchen looked very sad. They walked past the jail. The houses in the village of Grünheinchen, all except the Duke's, were made of wood and so was the jail. The walls were very thick and the only window was quite high, far above their heads.

Suddenly little Max said, "Look, there is a hole."

It was a large knothole in the wood. Max stood on his tiptoes and put his eye to the hole. "I can see him; I can see Old Hans. He is whittling just the way he always does."

"Oh, Max, let me see!" Gretchen stooped and, sure enough, she could see Old Hans—or part of him.

Max took out his pocket knife (every boy in Grünheinchen carried a knife) and scratched at the hole until he made it quite big. Then he put his lips to the hole and called shrilly, "Hans, Onkel Hans, come here. Come to the knothole."

Much astonished, Old Hans got up and followed the sound of the shrill, excited, small voice. The children gave him all the village news. He, in turn, told how long days were spent in jail.

"It will be a sad Christmas for you, Onkel Hans," said Gretchen. "We will miss you so at home."

"For us it will be worse, much worse." Max was almost crying. "We won't have any toys, not one."

Old Hans scratched his head. "You come back here tomorrow," he said.

The children could hardly wait until the next day. They went back to the knothole. "Here we are, here we are, Onkel Hans," they shouted.

Through the knothole which was now so big it had to be chinked with mud when not in use, Onkel Hans pushed a tiny wooden figure. It was a little boy carrying a flower in his hand.

"Oh," cried Max. "It's just like me."

"Only you never carry flowers," said Gretchen. "You just carry big sticks."

The next day a fat duck came through the knothole. Then a market woman. "Why," said Gretchen, "that is old Martha."

Day after day the tiny carved figures came through the knothole until the children had a whole village, and not one figure was more than three inches high.

"Onkel Hans has done so much for us. I wonder," sighed Gretchen, "can we make him a knothole Christmas dinner?"

They talked with their mother, and this is what they did. They wrapped some fine pieces of roast goose and chestnut stuffing into long thin bundles, four of them. They took some long, thin, spiced sausages that old Hans especially liked. Gretchen baked some rolls; they were a very funny shape, not very different from the sausages, long and thin. Even the Christmas cakes were rolled up tight with sugar and nuts and raisins inside.

"And a tall, skinny candle—like schoolmaster Egbert. I will make it myself—a Christmas candle," said Max. And he did from some beeswax he had gathered in the late summer and saved.

Christmas Eve came, with snow on the pointed roofs of the houses, on the pointed tops of the fir trees. Just as the lights were lit, Max and Gretchen went to the jail. They called Old Hans who came and gave them the prettiest toy of all, a funny, fat little figure with a star on his head, a Christmas angel. Then Max pushed and Gretchen pushed, and soon Hans's Christmas dinner was on a wooden plate that he held in his hands. Last of all, Max pushed through the candle.

"Made it myself," he said jumping up and down, "made it all myself."

The children said they had never had such toys, never, and they loved them because they were so tiny. And Hans said the best dinner he ever had was the Christmas dinner through a knothole.

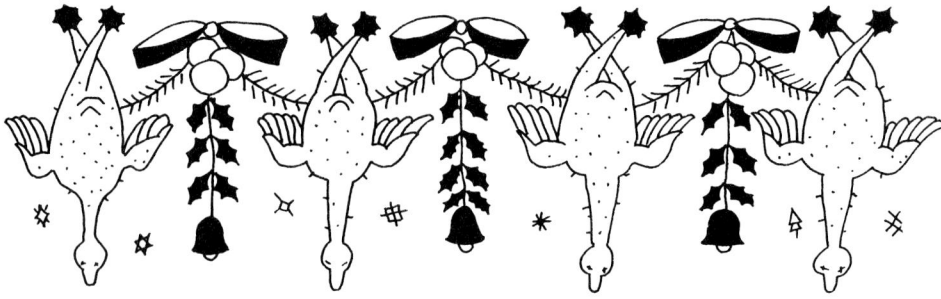

THE CRATCHITS' CHRISTMAS DINNER
Charles Dickens

Then up rose Mrs. Cratchit, Cratchit's wife, dressed out but poorly in a twice-turned gown, but brave in ribbons, assisted by Belinda Cratchit, second of her daughters, also brave in ribbons, while Master Peter Cratchit plunged a fork into the saucepan of potatoes. And now two smaller Cratchits, boy and girl, came tearing in, screaming that outside the baker's they had smelt the goose, and known it for their own.

"What has ever got your precious father, then?" said Mrs. Cratchit. "And your brother, Tiny Tim; and Martha warn't as late last Christmas Day by half an hour."

"Here's Martha, mother!" said a girl, appearing as she spoke.

"Here's Martha, mother!" cried the two young Cratchits. "Hurrah! There's such a goose, Martha!"

"Why, bless your heart alive, my dear, how late you are!" said Mrs. Cratchit, kissing her a dozen times, and taking off her shawl and bonnet for her with officious zeal.

"We'd a deal of work to finish up last night," replied the girl, "and had to clear away this morning, mother!"

"Well! Never mind so long as you are come," said Mrs. Cratchit. "Sit ye down before the fire, my dear, and have a warm, Lord bless ye!"

"No, no! There's father coming," cried the two young Cratchits, who were everywhere at once. "Hide, Martha, hide!"

So Martha hid herself, and in came little Bob, the father, with at least three feet of comforter, exclusive of the fringe, hanging down before him; and his threadbare clothes darned up and brushed, to look seasonable; and Tiny Tim upon his shoulder. Alas for Tiny Tim, he bore a little crutch, and had his limbs supported by an iron frame!

"Why, where's our Martha?" cried Bob Cratchit, looking round.

"Not coming," said Mrs. Cratchit.

"Not coming!" said Bob, with a sudden declension in his high spirits; for he had been Tim's blood horse all the way from church, and had come home rampant. "Not coming upon Christmas day!"

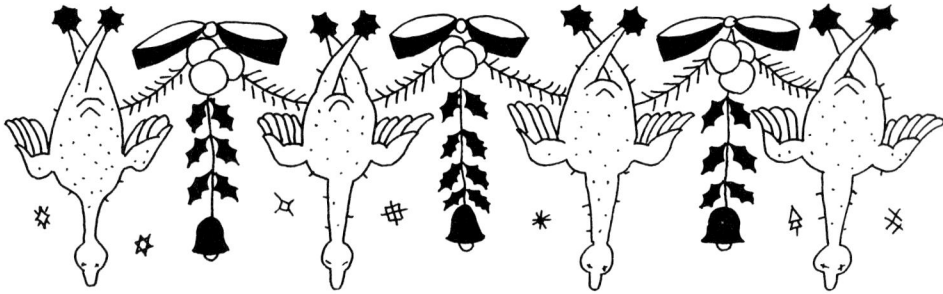

Martha didn't like to see him disappointed, if it were only in joke; so she came out prematurely from behind the closet door, and ran into his arms, while the two young Cratchits hustled Tiny Tim, and bore him off into the wash house, that he might hear the pudding singing in the copper.

"And how did little Tim behave?" asked Mrs. Cratchit, when she had rallied Bob on his credulity and Bob had hugged his daughter to his heart's content.

"As good as gold," said Bob, "and better. Somehow he gets thoughtful sitting by himself so much, and thinks the strangest things you ever heard. He told me, coming home, that he hoped the people saw him in the church, because he was a cripple, and it might be pleasant to them to remember upon Christmas Day who made lame beggars walk and blind men see."

Bob's voice was tremulous when he told them this, and trembled more when he said that Tiny Tim was growing strong and hearty.

His active little crutch was heard upon the floor, and back came Tiny Tim before another word was spoken, escorted by his brother and sister to his stool beside the fire; and while Bob, turning up his cuffs—as if, poor fellow, they were capable of being made more shabby—compounded some hot mixture in a jug with gin and lemons, and stirred it round and round and put it on the hob to simmer, Master Peter and the two ubiquitous young Cratchits went to fetch the goose, with which they soon returned in high procession.

Such a bustle ensued that you might have thought a goose the rarest of all birds, a feathered phenomenon, to which a black swan was a matter of course: and in truth it was something very like it in that house. Mrs. Cratchit made the gravy (ready beforehand in a little saucepan) hissing hot; Master Peter mashed the potatoes with incredible vigor; Miss Belinda sweetened up the apple sauce; Martha dusted the hot plates; Bob took Tiny Tim beside him in a tiny corner at the table; the two young Cratchits set chairs for everybody, not forgetting themselves, and mounting guard upon their posts, crammed spoons into their mouths, lest they should shriek for goose before their turn came to be helped. At last the dishes were set on, and grace was said. It was succeeded by a breathless pause as Mrs. Cratchit, looking slowly all along the carving knife, prepared to plunge it in the breast, but when she did, and when the long-expected gush of stuffing issued forth, one murmur of delight arose all round the board, and even Tiny Tim, excited by the two young Cratchits, beat on the table with the handle of his knife, and feebly cried, "Hurrah!"

There never was such a goose. Bob said he didn't believe there ever was such a goose cooked. Its tenderness and flavor, size and cheapness, were the themes of universal admiration. Eked out by the apple sauce and mashed potatoes, it was a sufficient dinner for the whole family; indeed, as Mrs. Cratchit said with great delight (surveying one small atom of a bone upon the dish), they hadn't ate it all at last! Yet every one had had enough, and the youngest Cratchits in particular were steeped in sage and onion to the eyebrows! But now, the plates being changed by Miss Belinda, Mrs. Cratchit left the room alone—too nervous to bear witness—to take the pudding up, and bring it in.

Suppose it should not be done enough! Suppose it should break in turning out! Suppose somebody should have got over the wall of the back yard and stolen it, while they were merry with the goose, a supposition at which the two young Cratchits became livid! All sorts of horrors were supposed.

Hallo! A great deal of steam! The pudding was out of the copper. A smell like a washing day! That was the cloth. A smell like an eating house and a pastry cook's next door to each other, with a laundress's next door to that! That was the pudding. In half a minute Mrs. Cratchit entered—flushed, but smiling proudly—with the pudding, like a speckled cannon ball, so hard and firm, blazing in half of half-a-quartern of ignited brandy, and bedight with Christmas holly stuck into the top.

Oh, a wonderful pudding! Bob Cratchit said, and calmly too, that he regarded it as the greatest success achieved by Mrs. Cratchit since their marriage. Mrs. Cratchit said that now the weight was off her mind, she would confess she had her doubts about the quantity of flour. Everybody had something to say about it, but nobody said or thought it was at all a small pudding for a large family. It would have been flat heresy to do so. Any Cratchit would have blushed to hint at such a thing.

At last the dinner was all done, the cloth was cleared, the hearth swept, and the fire made up. The compound in the jug being tasted and considered perfect, apples and oranges were put upon the table, and a shovelful of chestnuts on the fire. Then all the Cratchit family drew round the hearth, in what Bob Cratchit called a circle, meaning half a one; and at Bob Cratchit's elbow stood the family display of glass—two tumblers, and a custard cup without a handle. These held the hot stuff from the jug, however, as well as golden goblets would have done; and Bob served it out with beaming looks, while the chestnuts on the fire sputtered and cracked noisily. Then Bob proposed:

"A Merry Christmas to us all, my dears. God bless us!"

Which all the family re-echoed.

"God bless us every one!" said Tiny Tim, the last of all.

THE BOY WHO LAUGHED AT SANTA CLAUS

In Baltimore there lived a boy.
He wasn't anybody's joy.
Although his name was Jabez Dawes,
His character was full of flaws.
In school he never led the classes,
He hid old ladies' reading glasses,
His mouth was open while he chewed,
And elbows to the table glued.
He stole the milk of hungry kittens,
And walked through doors marked No Admittance.
He said he acted thus because
There wasn't any Santa Claus.
Another trick that tickled Jabez
Was crying "Boo!" at little babies.
He brushed his teeth, they said in town,
Sideways instead of up and down.
Yet people pardoned every sin
And viewed his antics with a grin
Till they were told by Jabez Dawes,
"There isn't any Santa Claus!"
Deploring how he did behave,
His parents quickly sought their grave.
They hurried through the portals pearly,
And Jabez left the funeral early.
Like whooping cough, from child to child,
He sped to spread the rumor wild:
"Sure as my name is Jabez Dawes
There isn't any Santa Claus!"
Slunk like a weasel or a marten
Through nursery and kindergarten,
Whispering low to every tot,
"There isn't any, no, there's not!
No beard, no pipe, no scarlet clothes,
No twinkling eyes, no cherry nose,
No sleigh, and furthermore, by Jiminy,
Nobody coming down the chimney!"
The children wept all Christmas Eve
And Jabez chortled up his sleeve.

No infant dared to hang up his stocking
For fear of Jabez' ribald mocking.
He sprawled on his untidy bed,
Fresh malice dancing in his head,
When presently with scalp a-tingling,
Jabez heard a distant jingling;
He heard the crunch of sleigh and hoof
Crisply alighting on the roof.
What good to rise and bar the door?
A shower of soot was on the floor.
Jabez beheld, oh, awe of awes,
The fireplace full of Santa Claus!

Then Jabez fell upon his knees
With cries of "Don't," and "Pretty please."
He howled, "I don't know where you read it.
I swear some other fellow said it!"
"Jabez," replied the angry saint,
"It isn't I, it's you that ain't.
Although there *is* a Santa Claus,
There isn't any Jabez Dawes!"
Said Jabez then with impudent vim,
"Oh, yes there is; and I am him!
Your language don't scare me, it doesn't—"
And suddenly he found he wasn't!
From grinning feet to unkempt locks
Jabez became a jack-in-the-box,
An ugly toy in Santa's sack,
Mounting the flue on Santa's back.
The neighbors heard his mournful squeal;
They searched for him, but not with zeal.
No trace was found of Jabez Dawes,
Which led to thunderous applause,
And people drank a loving cup
And went and hung their stockings up.
All you who sneer at Santa Claus,
Beware the fate of Jabez Dawes,
The saucy boy who told the saint off;
The child who got him, licked his paint off.

Ogden Nash

MY FIRST CHRISTMAS TREE
Hamlin Garland

I will begin by saying that we never had a Christmas tree in our house in the Wisconsin coulee; indeed, my father never saw one in a family circle till he saw that which I set up for my own children last year. But we celebrated Christmas in those days, always, and I cannot remember a time when we did not all hang up our stockings for "Sandy Claws" to fill. As I look back upon those days it seems as if the snows were always deep, the night skies crystal clear, and the stars especially lustrous with frosty sparkles of blue and yellow fire—and probably this was so, for we lived in a northern land where winter was usually stern and always long.

I recall one Christmas when "Sandy" brought me a sled, and a horse that stood on rollers—a wonderful tin horse which I very shortly split in two in order to see what his insides were. Father traded a cord of wood for the sled and the horse cost twenty cents—but they made the day wonderful.

Another notable Christmas Day, as I stood in our front yard, midleg deep in snow, a neighbor drove by closely muffled in furs, while behind his seat his son, a lad of twelve or fifteen, stood beside a barrel of apples, and as he passed he hurled a glorious big red one at me. It missed me, but bored a deep, round hole in the soft snow. I thrill yet with the remembered joy of burrowing for that delicious bomb. Nothing will ever smell quite as good as that Winesap of Northern Spy or whatever it was. It was a wayward impulse on the part of the boy in the sleigh, but it warms my heart after more than forty years.

We had no chimney in our home, but the stocking-hanging was a ceremony nevertheless. My parents, and especially my mother, entered into it with the best of humor. They always put up their own stockings or permitted us to do it for them and they always laughed next morning when they found potatoes or ears of corn in them. I can see now that my mother's laugh had a tear in it, for she loved pretty things and seldom got any during the years that we lived in the coulee.

When I was ten years old we moved and prospered in such ways that our stockings always held toys of some sort, and even my mother's stocking occasionally sagged with a simple piece of jewelry or a new comb or brush. But the thought of a family tree remained the luxury of millionaire city dwellers; indeed it was not till my fifteenth or sixteenth year that our Sunday school rose to the extravagance of a tree, and it is of this wondrous festival that I write.

The land about us was only partly cultivated at this time, and our district schoolhouse, a bare little box, was set bleakly on the prairie; but the Burr Oak Schoolhouse was not only larger, but it stood beneath great oaks as well and possessed the charm of a forest background through which a stream ran silently. It was our chief social center. There of a Sunday a regular preacher held "Divine service" with Sunday school as a sequence. At night—usually on Friday nights—the young people met in "ly-ceums," as we called them, to debate great questions or to "speak pieces" and read essays; and here it was that I saw my first Christmas tree.

I walked to that tree across four miles of moonlit snow. Snow? No, it was a floor of diamonds, a magical world, so beautiful that my heart still aches with the wonder of it and with the regret that it has all gone—gone with the keen eyes and the bounding pulse of the boy.

Our home at this time was a small frame house on the prairie almost directly west of the Burr

Oak grove, and as it was too cold to take the horses out my brother and I, with our tall boots, our visored caps, and our long woolen mufflers, started forth afoot defiant of the cold. We left the gate on the trot, bound for a sight of the glittering unknown. The snow was deep and we moved side by side in the grooves made by the hoofs of the horses, setting our feet in the shine left by the broad shoes of the wood sleighs whose going had smoothed the way for us. Our breaths rose like smoke in the still air. It must have been ten below zero, but that did not trouble us in those days, and at last we came in sight of the lights, in sound of the singing, the laughter, the bells of the feast.

It was a poor little building without tower or bell and its low walls had but three windows on a side, and yet it seemed very imposing to me that night as I crossed the threshold and faced the strange people who packed it to the door. I say "strange people" for though I had seen most of them many times they all seemed somehow alien to me that night. I was an irregular attendant at Sunday school and did not expect a present, therefore I stood against the wall and gazed with open-eyed marveling at the shining pine which stood where the pulpit was to be. I was made to feel the more embarrassed by reason of the remark of a boy who accused me of having forgotten to comb my hair.

This was not true, but the cap I wore always matted my hair down over my brow, and then, when I lifted it off, invariably disarranged it completely. Nevertheless I felt guilty—and hot. I don't suppose my hair was artistically barbered that night—I rather guess Mother had used the shears—and I can believe that I looked the half-wild colt that I was; but there was no call for that youth to direct attention to my unavoidable shagginess.

I don't think the tree had many candles, and I don't remember that it glittered with golden apples. But it was loaded with presents, and the girls coming and going clothed in bright garments made me forget my own looks—I think they made me forget to remove my overcoat, which was a sodden thing of poor cut and worse quality. I think I must have stood agape for nearly two hours listening to the songs, noting every motion of Adoniram Burtch and Asa Walker as they directed the ceremonies and prepared the way for the great event—that is to say, for the coming of Santa Claus himself.

A furious jingling of bells, a loud voice outside, the lifting of a window, the nearer clash of bells, and the dear old saint appeared (in the person of Stephen Bartle) clothed in a red robe, a belt of sleigh bells, and a long white beard. The children cried out, "Oh!" The girls tittered and shrieked with excitement, and the boys laughed and clapped their hands. Then "Sandy" made a little speech about being glad to see us all, but as he had many other places to visit, and as there were a great many presents to distribute, he guessed he'd have to ask some of the many pretty girls to help him. So he called upon Betty Burtch and Hattie Knapp—and I for one admired his taste, for they were the most popular maids of the school.

They came up blushing, and a little bewildered by the blaze of publicity thus blown upon them. But their native dignity asserted itself, and the distribution of the presents began. I have a notion now that the fruit upon the tree was mostly bags of popcorn and "corny copias" of candy, but as my brother and I stood there that night and saw everybody, even the rowdiest boy, getting something we felt aggrieved and rebellious. We forgot that we had come from afar—we only knew that we were being left out.

But suddenly, in the midst of our gloom, my brother's name was called, and a lovely girl with a gentle smile handed him a bag of popcorn. My heart glowed with gratitude. Somebody had thought of us; and when she came to me, saying sweetly, "Here's something for you," I had not words to thank her. This happened nearly forty years ago, but her smile, her outstretched hand, her sympathetic eyes are vividly before me as I write. She was sorry for the shock-headed boy who stood against the wall, and her pity made the little box of candy a casket of pearls. The fact that I swallowed the jewels on the road home does not take from the reality of my adoration.

At last I had to take my final glimpse of that wondrous tree, and I well remember the walk home. My brother and I traveled in wordless companionship. The moon was sinking toward the west, and the snow crust gleamed with a million fairy lamps. The sentinel watchdogs barked from lonely farmhouses, and the wolves answered from the ridges. Now and then sleighs passed us with lovers sitting two and two, and the bells on their horses had the remote music of romance to us whose boots drummed like clogs of wood upon the icy road.

Our house was dark as we approached and entered it, but how deliciously warm it seemed after the pitiless wind! I confess we made straight for the cupboard for a mince pie, a doughnut and a bowl of milk!

As I write this there stands in my library a thick-branched, beautifully tapering fir tree covered with the gold and purple apples of Hesperides, together with crystal ice points, green and red and yellow candles, clusters of gilded grapes, wreaths of metallic frost, and glittering angels swinging in ecstasy; but I doubt if my children will ever know the keen pleasure (that is almost pain) which came to my brother and to me in those Christmas days when an orange was not a breakfast fruit, but a casket of incense and of spice, a message from the sunlands of the South.

That was our compensation—we brought to our Christmastime a keen appetite and empty hands. And the lesson of it all is, if we are seeking a lesson, that it is better to give to those who want than to those for whom "we ought to do something because they did something for us last year."

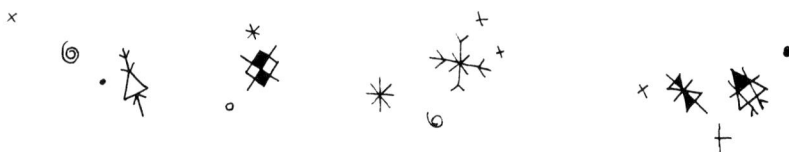

THE STARLIGHT NIGHT

Look at the stars! Look, look up at the skies!
　　O look at all the fire-folk sitting in the air!
　　The bright boroughs, the circle-citadels there!
Down in dim woods the diamond delves! the elves'-eyes!
The grey lawns cold where gold, where quickgold lies!
　　Wind-beat whitebeam! airy abeles set on a flare!
　　Flake-doves sent floating forth at a farmyard scare!—
Ah well! it is all a purchase, all is a prize.

Buy then! bid then!—What?—Prayer, patience, alms, vows.
Look, look: a May-mess, like on orchard boughs!
　　Look! March-bloom, like on mealed-with-yellow sallows!
These are indeed the barn; within doors house
The shocks. This piece-bright paling shuts the spouse
　　Christ home, Christ and His mother and all His hallows.

Gerard Manley Hopkins

26

A MISERABLE, MERRY CHRISTMAS

Lincoln Steffens

What interested me in our new neighborhood was not the school, nor the room I was to have in the house all to myself, but the stable which was built back of the house. My father let me direct the making of a stall, a little smaller than the other stalls, for my pony, and I prayed and hoped and my sister Lou believed that that meant that I would get the pony, perhaps for Christmas. I pointed out to her that there were three other stalls and no horses at all. This I said in order that she should answer it. She could not. My father, sounded, said that some day we might have horses and a cow; meanwhile the stable added to the value of a house. "Some day" is a pain to a boy who lives in and knows only "now." My good little sisters, to comfort me, remarked that Christmas was coming, but Christmas was always coming and grownups were always talking about it, asking you what you wanted and then giving you what they wanted you to have. Though everybody knew what I wanted, I told them all again. My mother knew that I told God, too, every night. I wanted a pony, and to make sure that they understood, I declared that I wanted nothing else.

"Nothing but a pony?" my father asked.

"Nothing," I said.

"Not even a pair of high boots?"

That was hard. I did want boots, but I stuck to the pony. "No, not even boots."

"Nor candy? There ought to be something to fill your stocking with, and Santa Claus can't put a pony into a stocking."

That was true, and he couldn't lead a pony down the chimney either. But no. "All I want is a pony," I said. "If I can't have a pony, give me nothing, nothing."

Now I had been looking myself for the pony I wanted, going to sales stables, inquiring of horsemen, and I had seen several that would do. My father let me "try" them. I tried so many ponies that I was learning fast to sit a horse. I chose several, but my father always found some fault with them. I was in despair. When Christmas was at hand I had given up all hope of a pony, and on Christmas Eve I hung up my stocking along with my sisters, of whom, by the way, I now had three. . . . They were so happy that Christmas came that I caught some of their merriment. I speculated on what I'd get; I hung up the biggest stocking I had, and we all went reluctantly to bed to wait till morning. Not to sleep; not right away. We were told that we must not only go to sleep promptly; we must not wake up till seven-thirty the next morning—or if we did, we must not go to the fireplace for our Christmas. Imposible.

We did sleep that night, but we woke up at six A.M. We lay in our beds and debated through the open doors whether to obey till, say, half-past six. Then we bolted. I don't know who started it, but there was a rush. We all disobeyed; we raced to disobey and get first to the fireplace in the front room downstairs. And there they were, the gifts, all sorts of wonderful things, mixed-up piles of presents; only, as I disentangled the mess, I saw that my stocking was empty; it hung limp; not a thing in it; and under and around it—nothing. My sisters had knelt down each by her pile of gifts; they were squealing with delight, till they looked up and saw me standing there in my nightgown with nothing. They left their piles to come to me and look with me at my empty place. Nothing. They felt my stocking: nothing.

I don't remember whether I cried at that moment, but my sisters did. They ran with me back to my bed, and there we all cried till I became indignant. That helped some. I got up, dressed, and driving my sistes away, I went alone out into the yard, down to the stable, and there, all by myself, I wept. My mother came out to me by and by; she found me in my pony stall, sobbing on the floor, and she tried to comfort me. But I heard my father outside; he had come part way with her, and she was having some sort of angry quarrel with him. She tried to comfort me; besought me to come to

27

breakfast. She left me and went on into the house with sharp words for my father.

I don't know what kind of breakfast the family had. My sisters said it was "awful." They were ashamed to enjoy their own toys. They came to me, and I was rude; I ran away from them. I went around to the front of the house, sat down on the steps, and, the crying over, I ached. I was wronged, I was hurt—I can feel now what I felt then, and I am sure that if one could see the wounds upon our hearts, there would be found still upon mine a scar from that terrible Christmas morning. And my father, the practical joker, he must have been hurt, too, a little. I saw him looking out of the window. He was watching me or something for an hour or two, drawing back the curtain ever so little lest I catch him, but I saw his face, and I think I can see now the anxiety upon it, the worried impatience.

After—I don't know how long—surely an hour or two—I was brought to the climax of my agony by the sight of a man riding a pony down the street, a pony and a brand-new saddle; the most beautiful saddle I ever saw, and it was a boy's saddle; the man's feet were not in the stirrups; his legs were too long. The outfit was perfect; it was the realization of all my dreams, the answer to all my prayers. A fine new bridle, with a light curb bit. And the pony! As he drew near, I saw that the pony was really a small horse, what we called an Indian pony, a bay, with black mane and tail, and one white foot and a white star on his forehead. For such a horse as that I would have given, I could have forgiven, anything.

But the man, a disheveled fellow with a blackened eye and a fresh-cut face, came along, reading the numbers on the houses, and, as my hopes—my impossible hopes—rose, he looked at our door and passed by, he and the pony, and the saddle and the bridle. Too much. I fell upon the steps, and having wept before, I broke now into such a flood of tears that I was a floating wreck when I heard a voice.

"Say, kid," it said, "do you know a boy named Lennie Steffens?"

I looked up. It was the man on the pony, back again, at our horse block.

"Yes," I spluttered through my tears. "That's me."

"Well," he said, "then this is your horse. I've been looking all over for you and your house. Why don't you put your number where it can be seen?"

"Get down," I said, running out to him.

He went on saying something about "ought to have got here at seven o'clock; he told me to bring the nag here and tie him to your post and leave him for you . . ."

"Get down," I said.

He got down, and he boosted me up to the saddle. He offered to fit the stirrups to me, but I didn't want him to. I wanted to ride.

"What's the matter with you?" he said, angrily. "What are you crying for? Don't you like the horse? He's a dandy, this horse. I know him of old. He's fine at cattle; he'll drive 'em alone."

I hardly heard, I could scarcely wait, but he persisted. He adjusted the stirrups, and then, finally, off I rode, slowly, at a walk, so happy, so thrilled, that I did not know what I was doing. I did not look back at the house or the man; I rode off up the street, taking note of everything—of the reins, of the pony's long mane, of the carved leather saddle. I had never seen anything as beautiful. And mine! I was going to ride up past Miss Kay's house. But I noticed on the horn of the saddle some stains like raindrops, so I turned and trotted home, not to the house but to the stable. There was the family, father, mother, sisters, all working for me, all happy. They had been putting in place the tools of my new business: blankets, currycomb, brush, pitchfork—everything, and there was hay in the loft.

"What did you come back so soon for?" somebody asked. "Why didn't you go on riding?"

I pointed to the stains. "I wasn't going to get my new saddle rained on," I said. And my father laughed. "It isn't raining," he said. "Those are not raindrops."

"They are tears," my mother gasped, and she gave my father a look which sent him off to the house. Worse still, my mother offered to wipe away the tears still running out of my eyes. I gave her such a look as she had given him, and she went off after my father, drying her own tears.

My sisters remained and we all unsaddled the pony, put on his halter, led him to his stall, tied and fed him. It began really to rain; so all the rest of that memorable day we curried and combed that pony. The girls plaited his mane, forelock, and tail, while I pitchforked hay to him and curried and brushed, curried and brushed. For a change we brought him out to drink; we led him up and down, blanketed like a race horse; we took turns at that. But the best, the most inexhaustible fun, was to clean him.

When we went reluctantly to our midday Christmas dinner, we smelt of horse, and my sisters had to wash their faces and hands. I was asked to, but I wouldn't, till my mother bade me look in the mirror. Then I washed up—quick. My face was caked with muddy lines of tears that had coursed over my cheeks to my mouth. Having washed away that shame, I ate my dinner, and as I ate I grew hungrier and hungrier. It was my first meal that day, and as I filled up on the turkey and stuffing, the cranberries and the pies, the fruit and the nuts—as I swelled, I could laugh. My mother said I still choked and sobbed now and then, but I laughed, too; I saw and enjoyed my sisters' presents till—I had to go out and attend to my pony, who was there, really and truly there, the promise, the beginning, of a happy double life. And—I went and looked to make sure—there was the saddle, too, and the bridle.

But that Christmas, which my father had planned so carefully, was it the best or the worst I ever knew? He often asked me that; I never could answer as a boy. I think now that it was both. It covered the whole distance from broken-hearted misery to bursting happiness—too fast. A grownup could hardly have stood it.

SANTA CLAUS

On wool-soft feet he peeps and creeps,
　　while in the moon-blanched snow,
Tossing their sled-belled antlered heads,
　　His reindeer wait below.
Bright eyes, peaked beard, and bulging sack,
　　He stays to listen, and look, because
A child lies sleeping out of sight.
　　Oh yes! It's Santa Claus.

Walter de la Mare

KEEPING CHRISTMAS WITH MARK TWAIN

Christmas was a festive occasion at the home of the Samuel Clemens family. Dickens might well have said of them that they were people who knew how to keep Christmas. The first account is by Katy Leary who worked in the service of the household for twenty-nine years. The next is by Mark Twain's second daughter, Clara. The last selection is excerpted from Twain's autobiography completed shortly before his death in the spring of 1910. Jean Clemens, Mark Twain's youngest daughter, died December 24, 1909.

The Christmases they used to have was something wonderful. The way they used to make everybody happy! Baskets and packages all over the place. Mrs. Clemens would be fixing baskets in the Billiard Room off the library (they always used to do the Christmas things there) and she used to do up about fifty baskets herself. She always had a crowd of people, children and old people and grown-up people, too, depending on her and she fixed them up wonderful baskets with a big turkey and cans of peas and tomatoes and vegetables and then, oh, a bottle of wine and a great big box of candy, and nuts and raisins, and then there was always some stockings and underwear and a few pretty things, too. She used to give every one of them a present, individual-like, extra. She knew, it seems to me, just what each person wanted most and she shopped for weeks before Christmas, doing up all those things and having all those baskets ready, and then when Christmas morning come, if it was cold and snow on the ground, Mr. Clemens would start out to distribute the things. He'd put on his big fur overcoat, take the sleigh and the two children with him, Susy and Clara, and they'd start early in the morning with them great baskets. The children would read the names and then Mr. Clemens would lift out the baskets and Patrick would take them into the house.

Mr. Clemens looked just like Santa Claus, you know, with that great big fur coat with a white fur collar on it, and he and the children had such fun over it.

Katy Leary

The day before Christmas was always spent in a somewhat fatiguing way by my sisters and me. We drove around with the coachman while he delivered Christmas packages that went to the poor. Great baskets with the feet of turkeys protruding below blankets of flowers and fruit. Wrapped up in mufflers and snugly tucked in a fur robe, we children drove far out into the country in an open sleigh, tingling with delight at the sound of the bells.

When Christmas Eve arrived at last, we children hung up our stockings in the schoolroom next to our nursery, and did it with great ceremony. Mother always recited the thrilling little poem, "'Twas the night before Christmas, when all through the house," etc. Father sometimes dressed up as Santa Claus and, after running about a dimly lighted room (we always turned the gas down low), trying to warm himself after the cold drive through the snow, he sat down and told some of his experiences on the way.

His little talk usually ended with words something like these: "As I often lose the letters I receive, or get them mixed up, I may have confused all your wishes, so that the stocking which should have bulged out with a donkey's head may be depressed by a hair-ribbon. Therefore, I should like to gather up your thanks now, as you may not feel like giving me any after Christmas. Anyway, I shall be gone then."

We all squealed, "Thank you, thank you, Santa Claus, for the things we hope to like," and then after a short game of tag Father ran away to remove his cotton beard and red coat.

At this time my sisters and I were obliged to retire at an early hour every evening, not excepting Christmas Eve. Therefore, by eight o'clock we were in bed, launched on a long night of

wakefulness, while mother started on a night of work down in the "mahogany room." Two of us, Jean and I, slept in the nursery, and my elder sister, Susy, occupied a little blue room adjoining. But, on Christmas Eve, Susy crept into bed with me and we listened for the mysterious sounds that would betray the presence of fairies in the schoolroom.

"Ah, there they are! rattling paper, subdued voices. A dull thud; something falls. I wonder what it is? If only it isn't broken! Oh, Susy, listen to that heavy thing they are dragging across the floor! What on earth can that be? I'll die if I can't find out soon. How many hours yet? If only we could sleep!"

Finally all became still in the schoolroom. The fairies must have gone. Not a sound. The forms left behind are motionless, speechless. . . .

By and by, Susy whispered to me, "Let's take *one* little peek through the door. With a tiny bit of light from the bathroom we might get an idea of the shapes without seeing anything."

It didn't take me long to say "Yes."

Opening the door a few inches, and by means of a dim ray of light, we saw—

"Oh dear! Shut the door quick! We must not look. That's wicked. What do you suppose that huge black thing can be? It seems to fill the room. Come, let's try to go to sleep." Of course that was impossible.

Eventually 6 a.m. came and we rang for the nurse to build a fire in the schoolroom and help us dress with as little washing as possible. And now the door opens wide! . . .

At last each makes a rush for her own table, scattering ribbons, papers, and ejaculations with vehement haste. . . . The big object seeming to fill the center of the room turns out to be a lovely upright piano. Can it be true? . . .

Father and Mother always rose very late on Christmas morning, having spent most of the night up. So we were well acquainted with our presents, and had even written several letters of thanks before our parents appeared. They inspected their gifts, which were down in the drawing-room and callers from the neighborhood began to arrive.

Clara Clemens

I have been to Jean's parlor. Such a turmoil of Christmas presents for servants and friends! They are everywhere; tables, chairs, sofas, the floor—everything is occupied and overoccupied. It is many and many a year since I have seen the like. In that ancient day Mrs. Clemens and I used to slip softly into the nursery at midnight on Christmas Eve and look the array of presents over. The children were little then. And now here is Jean's parlor looking just as that nursery used to look. The presents are not labeled—the hands are forever idle that would have labeled them today. Jean's mother always worked herself down with her Christmas preparations. Jean did the same yesterday and the preceding days, and the fatigue has cost her her life. The fatigue caused the convulsion that attacked her this morning. She had had no attack for months.

On a shelf I found a pile of my books and I knew what it meant. She was waiting for me to come home from Bermuda and autograph them, then she would send them away. If I only knew whom she intended them for! But I shall never know. I will keep them.

And in a closet she had hidden a surprise for me—a thing I have often wished I owned; a noble big globe. I couldn't see it for the tears. She will never know the pride I take in it, and the pleasure. Today the mails are full of loving remembrances for her: full of those old, old kind words she loved so well, "Merry Christmas to Jean!" If she could only have lived one day longer! God rest her sweet spirit.

Mark Twain, Christmas Day, 1909

CHRISTMAS OF THE LONG AGO

You could feel its stir an' hum
Weeks an' weeks before it come;
Somethin' in the atmosphere
Told you when the day was near,
Didn't need no almanacs;
That was one o' Nature's fac's.
Every cottage decked out gay—
Cedar wreaths an' holly spray—
An' the stores, how they were drest,
Tinsel tell you couldn't rest;
Every winder fixed up pat,

Candy canes, an' things like that,
Noah's arks, an' guns, an' dolls,
An' all kinds o' fol-de-rols.
Then with frosty bells a-chime,
Slidin' down the hills o' time,
Right amidst the fun an' din
Christmas come a-bustlin' in,
Raised his cheery voice to call
Out a welcome to us all;
Hale and hearty, strong an' bluff,
That was Christmas, sure enough.

Paul Laurence Dunbar

HOW COME SANTA CLAUS AND CHRISTMAS AND ALL
Roark Bradford

Have you ever wondered how Santa Claus came to be associated with Christmas? In this Christmas fable a storyteller fashions a warm and humorous yarn in response to the queries of young listeners. This story, in the folk tradition of the "trickster tale," was also republished recently in *Christmas Gif', An Anthology of Christmas Poems, Songs, and Stories, Written By and About African Americans.*

You see, one time hit was a little baby bawned name' de Poor Little Jesus, but didn't nobody know dat was his name yit. Dey knew he was a powerful smart and powerful purty little baby, but dey didn't know his name was de Poor Little Jesus. So, 'cause he was so smart and so purty, ev'ybody thought he was gonter grow up and be de kaing. Now, kaings was bad fo'ks. Dey was mean. Dey'd druther kill you den leave you alone. You see a kaing wawkin' down de road, and you better light out across de field, 'cause de kaing would wawk up and chop yo' haid off. And de law couldn't tech him, cause he was de kaing. So quick as dat news got spread around, ev'ybody jest about bust to git on de good side er de baby, 'cause dey figure efn dey start soon enough he'd grow up likin' 'em and not chop dey haids off.

So old Moses went over and give him a hund'ed dollars in gold. And old Methuselah went over and give him a diamond ring. And old Peter give him a fine white silk robe. And ev'ybody was runnin' in wid fine presents so de Poor Little Jesus wouldn't grow up and chop de haids off.

Ev'ybody but old Sandy Claus. Old Sandy Claus was kind er old and didn't git around much, and he didn't hyar de news dat de Poor Little Jesus was gonter grow up and be de kaing. So him and de old lady was settin' back by de fire one night, toastin' dey shins and tawkin' about dis and dat, when old Miz Sandy Claus up and remark, she say, "Sandy, I hyars Miss Mary got a brand new baby overt at her house."

"Is dat a fack?" says Sandy Claus. "Well, well, hit's a mighty cold night to do anything like dat, ain't hit? But on de yuther hand, he'll be a heap er pleasure and fun for her next summer I reckon."

So de tawk went on, and finally old Sandy Claus remark dat hit was powerful lonesome around de house since all er de chilluns growed up and married off.

"Dey all married well," say Miz Sandy Claus, "and so I say, 'Good ruddance.' You ain't never had to git up and cyore dey colic and mend dey clothes, so you gittin' lonesome. Me, I love 'em all, but I'm glad dey's married and doin' well."

So de tawk run on like dat for a while, and den old Sandy Claus got up and got his hat. "I b'lieve," he say, "I'll drap over and see how dat baby's gittin' along. I ain't seed no chillun in so long I'm pyore hongry to lean my eyes up agin a baby."

"You ain't goin' out on a night like dis, is you?" say Miz Sandy Claus.

"Sho I'm goin' out on a night like dis," say Sandy Claus. "I'm pyore cravin' to see some chilluns."

"But hit's snowin' and goin' on," say Miz Sandy Claus. "You know yo' phthisic been develin' you, anyhow, and you'll git de chawley mawbuses sloppin' around in dis weather."

"No mind de tawk," say Sandy Claus. "Git me my umbrella and my overshoes. And you better git me a little somethin' to take along for a cradle gift, too, I reckon."

"You know hit ain't nothin' in de house for no cradle gift," say Miz Sandy Claus.

"Git somethin'," say Sandy Claus. "You got to give a new baby somethin', or else you got bad luck. Get me one er dem big red apples outn de kitchen."

"What kind er cradle gift is an apple?" say Miz Sandy Claus. "Don't you reckon dat baby git all de apples he want?"

"Git me de apple," say Sandy Claus. "Hit ain't much, one way you looks at hit. But f'm de way dat baby gonter look at de apple, hit'll be a heap."

So Sandy Claus got de apple and he lit out.

Well, when he got to Miss Mary's house ev'ybody was standin' around givin' de Poor Little Jesus presents. Fine presents. Made outn gold and silver and diamonds and silk, and all like dat. Dey had de presents stacked around dat baby so high you couldn't hardly see over 'em. So when ev'ybody seed old Sandy Claus come in dey looked to see what he brang. And when dey seed he didn't brang nothin' but a red apple, dey all laughed.

"Quick as dat boy grows up and gits to be de kaing," dey told him, "he gonter chop yo' haid off."

"No mind dat," say Sandy Claus. "Ya'll jest stand back." And so he went up to de crib and he pushed away a handful er gold and silver and diamonds and stuff, and handed de Poor Little Jesus dat red apple. "Hyar, son," he say, "take dis old apple. See how she shines?"

And de Poor Little Jesus reached up and grabbed dat apple in bofe hands, and laughed jest as brash as you please!

Den Sandy Claus tuck and tickled him under de chin wid his before finger, and say, "Goodly-goodly-goodly." And de Poor Little Jesus laughed some more and he reached up and grabbed a fist full er old Sandy Claus' whiskers, and him and old Sandy Claus went round and round!

So about dat time, up stepped de Lawd. "I swear, old Sandy Claus," say de Lawd. "Betwixt dat apple and dem whiskers, de Poor Little Jesus ain't had so much fun since he been bawn."

So Sandy Claus stepped back and bowed low and give de Lawd hy-dy, and say, "I didn't know ev'ybody was chiv-areein', or else I'd a stayed at home. I didn't had nothin' much to bring dis time, 'cause you see how hit's been dis year. De dry weather and de bull weevils got mighty nigh all de cotton, and de old lady been kind er puny—"

"Dat's all right, Sandy," say de Lawd. "Gold and silver have I a heap of. But verily you sho do know how to handle yo'se'f around de chilluns."

"Well, Lawd," say Sandy Claus, "I don't know much about chilluns. Me and de old lady raised up fou'teen. But she done most er de work. Me, I jest likes 'em and I manages to git along wid 'em."

"You sho do git along wid 'em good," say de Lawd.

"Hit's easy to do what you likes to do," say Sandy Claus.

"Well," say de Lawd, "hit might be somethin' in dat, too. But de trouble wid my world is, hit ain't enough people which likes to do de right thing. But you likes to do wid chilluns, and dat's what I needs. So stand still and shet yo' eyes whilst I passes a miracle on you."

So Sandy Claus stood still and shet his eyes, and de Lawd r'ared back and passed a miracle on him and say, "Old Sandy Claus, live forever, and make my chilluns happy."

So Sandy Claus opened his eyes and say, "Thank you kindly, Lawd. But do I got to keep 'em happy all de time? Dat's a purty big job. Hit'd be a heap er fun, but still and at de same time—"

"Yeah, I knows about chilluns, too," say de Lawd. "Chilluns got to fret and git in devilment ev'y now and den and git a whuppin' f'm dey maw, or else dey skin won't git loose so's dey kin grow. But you just keep yo' eyes on 'em and make 'em all happy about once a year. How's dat?"

"Dat's fine," Say Sandy Claus. "Hit'll be a heap er fun, too. What time er de year you speck I better make 'em happy, Lawd?"

"Christmas suit me," say de Lawd, "efn hit's all okay wid you."

"Hit's jest about right for me," say old Sandy Claus.

So ev'y since dat day and time old Sandy Claus been clawin' de chilluns on Christmas, and dat's on de same day dat de Poor Little Jesus got bawned. 'Cause dat's de way de Lawd runs things. O' cou'se de Lawd knowed hit wa'n't gonter be long before de Poor Little Jesus growed up and got to be a man. And when he done dat, all de grown fo'ks had him so's dey c'd moan they sins away and lay they burdens down on him, and git happy in they hearts. De Lawd made Jesus for de grown fo'ks. But de Lawd know de chilluns got to have some fun, too, so dat's how come hit's Sandy Claus and Christmas and all.

THE WOODEN SHOES OF LITTLE WOLFF
François Coppée

Once upon a time, so long ago that the world has forgotten the date, in a city in the north of France, there was a little boy just seven years old whose name was Wolff. He was an orphan and lived with his aunt, a hard-hearted old woman, who never kissed him but once a year, on New Year's Day; and who sighed with regret every time she gave him a bowlful of soup.

But little Wolff was naturally so good that he loved the old woman just the same, although she frightened him very much. He could never look at her without trembling, for fear she would scold him.

Wolff's aunt was known through all the village to have a stocking full of money in the house, but she made Wolff wear very old and ragged clothes. The schoolmaster, who liked best those pupils who were well dressed, was very unkind to Wolff and often punished him unjustly. The other pupils, too, made fun of Wolff's ill-fitting clothes. The poor little fellow, therefore, was as miserable as the stones in the street, and when Christmas came hid himself in out-of-the-way corners to cry.

On the Eve of the great Day the schoolmaster was to take all his pupils to the midnight mass.

Now as the winter was very severe, and a quantity of snow had fallen within the past few days, the boys came to the place of meeting warmly wrapped up, with fur-lined caps drawn down over their ears, padded jackets, gloves and knitted mittens, and good strong boots with thick soles. Only little Wolff presented himself shivering in his thin everyday clothes, and wearing on his feet socks and wooden shoes.

His thoughtless comrades made a thousand jests about his rough dress, but little Wolff was so occupied in trying to keep warm that he took no notice of them. Then the band of boys, marching two by two, started for the parish church.

It was comfortable inside the church, which was brilliant with lighted tapers. And the pupils, made lively by the gentle warmth, the sound of the organ, and the singing of the choir, began to chatter in low tones. They boasted of the fine suppers that were awaiting them at home. They talked about what the Christ Child would bring them, or what he would leave in their shoes which they would certainly be careful to place before the fire when they went to bed. And the eyes of the little rogues, lively as a crowd of mice, sparkled with delight as they thought of the many gifts they would find on waking,—the pink bags of burnt almonds, the bonbons, lead soldiers standing in rows, menageries, and magnificent jumping-jacks, dressed in purple and gold.

Little Wolff knew well that his stingy old aunt would send him to bed without any supper; but as he had been good and industrious all the year, he trusted that the Christ Child would not forget him. So he, too, looked forward to putting his wooden shoes in the ashes of the fireplace.

The midnight mass was ended. The worshipers hurried away: The band of pupils following the schoolmaster, passed out of the church.

Now, under the porch, seated on a stone bench, was a child asleep. The child was dressed in a garment of white linen but his feet were bare despite the cold. He was not a beggar, for his robe was clean and new, and beside him upon the ground, tied in a cloth, were the tools of a carpenter's apprentice.

The pupils so warmly clad and shod, passed heedlessly by the unknown child. Some even looked with scorn on the barefooted one. But little Wolff, coming last out of the church, stopped deeply moved before the sleeping child.

"Alas!" said the orphan to himself, "how dreadful! This poor little one goes without stockings in weather so cold! And, what is worse, he has not even a shoe to set out while he sleeps, so that the Christ Child may put something there to comfort him in his misery."

So, out of the goodness of his heart, little Wolff drew off the wooden shoe from his right foot and placed it before the sleeping child. Then limping along with only one shoe and wetting his sock in the snow he returned to his aunt.

"Look at that worthless fellow!" cried his aunt. "What have you done with your wooden shoe, you little wretch?"

Little Wolff did not know how to deceive. Although he was shaking with terror, he tried to stammer out some account of the good deed he had done.

But the old woman laughed scornfully.

"Ah, this young man thinks he is rich enough to give away his wooden shoe to beggars! That is something new! Well, since you are so generous, I am going to put the remaining shoe in the chimney, and I promise you the Christ Child will leave something there to whip you with in the morning. And you shall pass the day tomorrow on dry bread and water. We shall see if you give away your shoe next time to the first vagabond that comes along."

And saying this the wicked woman gave him a box on each ear, and made him climb to his room in the loft. There, grieved to the heart, he lay down in the darkness and fell asleep, his pillow wet with tears.

But in the morning, when the old woman went downstairs, what a wonderful sight met her eyes! She saw the great chimney full of beautiful playthings, and sacks of delicious candies, and all sorts of good things. And there, to her surprise she saw the right shoe—the one that her nephew had given to the little waif, standing by the side of the left shoe which she herself had put there.

"Goodness gracious!" the aunt exclaimed in unbelief.

Little Wolff, hearing his aunt's exclamation, ran downstairs and stood in ecstasy before all the splendid presents.

Suddenly there were loud peals of laughter out-of-doors. The old woman and the little boy hurried outside, where all the neighbors were gathered around the public fountain. What had happened? Oh, something very amusing and very extraordinary! The children of all the wealthy people of the village, those whose parents had wished to surprise them with the most beautiful gifts, had found only sticks in their shoes.

Then the orphan and the old woman, thinking of all the beautiful things that were in their chimney, were full of amazement. Presently they saw the priest coming toward them, wonderingly. In the church porch, where a child, clad in a white robe and with bare feet, had rested his sleeping head the evening before, the priest had just found a circle of gold incrusted with precious stones.

The people realized then that the beautiful sleeping child, with the carpenter's tools beside him, was the Christ Child himself, become for an hour such as he was when he had worked in his parents' house. And they bowed their heads before the miracle that the good God had seen fit to work, to reward the faith and charity of little Wolff.

SHEPHERD'S SONG AT CHRISTMAS

Look there at the star!
I, among the least,
Will arise and take
A journey to the East.
But what shall I bring
As a present for the King?
What shall I bring to the Manger?

I will bring a song,
A song that I will sing,
A song for the King
In the Manger.

Watch out for my flocks,
Do not let them stray.
I am going on a journey
Far, far away.
But what shall I bring
As a present for the Child?
What shall I bring to the Manger?

I will bring a lamb.
Gentle, meek, and mild,
A lamb for the Child
In the Manger.

I'm just a shepherd boy,
Very poor I am—
But I know there is
A King in Bethlehem.
What shall I bring
As a present just for Him?
What shall I bring to the Manger?

I will bring my heart
And give my heart to Him.
I will give my heart
To the Manger.

Langston Hughes

BABUSHKA
Katharine Gibson

Late one snowy night in Russia, more than nineteen hundred years ago, Babushka was sweeping her house. She was the best housekeeper in the village. And though she lived all by herself, her little cottage was as bright as a new kopek. Even though it was winter, flowers bloomed on her window sill. Her painted walls were as gay as when the colors were still wet, her carved doorway, her carved bed, her little carved chairs were waxed and polished until they shone like the soft satin of some great lady's gown. From morn to sundown Babushka was at work in her tiny house, so it is no wonder that she was sweeping late at night.

When she had finished she opened her door to brush the snow from her sill. The moon shone brightly, the snow lay heaped like silver and the ice of the river gleamed like a string of brilliant crystals. The wind blew sharply; it cut through Babushka's little furred dress and nipped her ears and nose until they were scarlet.

Suddenly a warmth came into the wind; it seemed like a spring breeze; it was filled with the most delicious fragrance. "What could it be?" Babushka wondered. "Where does it come from?"

She looked down the road. There in the shining moonlight was the most marvelous procession she had ever seen. First there came an outrider on a strange, long-legged, humped beast which she later learned was a camel. The outrider had a long curved sword. His mantle was of scarlet. Silently he came; his beast's padded feet made no noise. Following him was an endless line of horsemen all arrayed in strange armor from the east. Each of these was followed by a servant bearing a torch. The torch flared out dimly in the moonlight. The hoofs of the horses sank deeply into the snow. They were also silent.

Behind the riders came carts filled with all manner of folk, dressed as gayly as gypsies though they were in silks and cloth of gold, not in rags. They had tents striped red and blue, finely woven rugs; they had cooking pots of brass and copper rimmed with silver, dishes of silver, and jeweled drinking cups. All of these flashed brilliantly. Babushka could hardly believe her wondering eyes. On came the procession; cart after cart sank into the deep snow; silently they moved. At last the end! There rode Three Men, the most wonderful she had ever gazed upon.

One was little and old, he had gray hair beneath his turban, his beard was gray, but his dim eyes were young with watching. He was dressed from head to foot in a garment of gold, the color of the rising sun.

One was somewhat taller and younger; his eyes were bright; his hair curled crisply. He was robed in silk the color of evening, violet and purple.

Then came the Third. Never in all her life had Babushka seen any man so tall. His face was as beautiful as though it had been cut from an old coin; his skin was black. He was an Ethiopian. He was wearing the color of the noonday sun, orange and flame.

The First of the three held gold in his hand; the Second and Third had small caskets from which issued the warm, delicious fragrance that had first greeted Babushka's eager nostrils.

Babushka lifted her eyes to the Three. At first they did not see her. The Ethiopian was pointing to the heavens; the others were looking where he pointed. Babushka gazed too. Right above the Three was a star. It was so bright that it dazzled Babushka's eyes. Even the moon seemed pale beside its marvelous, streaming rays. As Babushka stood there in front of her door in her little furred gown, with the light from the lamps making a crown of her dark braids, she was very fair. The First Man gave a signal; the whole procession stopped; as it did so, the star stood still above them. The Second spoke.

"Do you watch the star, also?"

Babushka was so amazed and so filled by the music of his voice that she could only bow and curtsy.

"It leads us to the King," said the First.

"Will you not go with us?" spoke the Ethiopian. "We will carry you safely to our Lord and you shall look upon His face."

Babushka's eyes fell upon her broom. Suddenly for the space of a single sentence she found the use of her tongue.

"Oh no, sir, thank you, sir, I cannot leave my house, sir. Why it takes me all day long to brush and sweep it."

The Third looked upon her with pity in his eyes; the First gave the signal. The procession moved on silently through the snow. Babushka stood and watched until its last shining jewel had passed from sight.

The next morning, when she awoke, it seemed to her all a dream. Surely the great Kings had not come; surely she had not refused to follow them. As swiftly as could be, she jumped from her bed.

A bit of ash had fallen on the hearth. Babushka looked for her broom. No, it was not in the corner; no, it was not in the cupboard; no, it had not fallen behind the stove. Where was her broom? Then she remembered. Her broom, why she was sweeping the sill with it when the Three, when the dream came. She opened the door. There almost buried was her broom. All through the night the snow had been falling; all the foot-prints and the tracks of the carts had been hidden, but there was her broom.

Babushka stepped inside. How sweet her little house smelled. What could it be? Why, it was Babushka herself. The Ethiopian King had dropped a bit of his precious myrrh upon her sleeve. The tears filled Babushka's eyes. It had not been a dream. She *had* left her broom there. She still bore the marvelous fragrance. They had come and gone.

At that thought Babushka was filled with a kind of madness. They had gone to see the King. She would hurry, she would find them, she would catch up with them. All her life she would search until she looked into the face of the King. Babushka threw down her broom, wrapped her cape about her, and without waiting for her boots ran out the door.

The days passed, and the years. Babushka hunted and searched. Her dark hair became gray, then white. Her little house was half filled with snow. She was as likely to run out leaving her door open as to close it. The paint was dull, the furniture marred, mats of cobweb lay in the corners, the hearth was strewn with ashes. Babushka was searching, searching, searching. . . .

One day she met a man who told her that after thirteen days the Three Men of the Orient had reached their goal and departed again. They had found the King. He was a Child born in a stable, wrapped in swaddling clothes and lying in a manger.

When Babushka heard that the King was a Child, her heart swelled and nearly broke with longing. "I must find him, I must hunt," she said. On and on she rushed, mile after mile. Wherever she saw a child, she looked long into his face. All her savings she spent for toys and sweets.

Sometimes a nurse or mother would come at night into the nursery, hearing the baby of the house crow and gurgle. There bending above him they would catch a glimpse of a strange old figure with young eyes. Like a breath of wind, she would be gone. In the morning, a bright carved chicken or a tiny duck would be lying in the child's crib.

44

"Ah," the nurse or mother would say, "Babushka has been here."

"Ah," all the children would cry, "Babushka was in this very room last night."

One day Babushka met a traveler who told her that the King had grown to be a man long ago, and that long ago he had died upon the tree. When she heard this, Babushka cried out with pain. The Child was a Man; the Child no longer lived; she would *never* find Him. But soon she half forgot this. More and more clearly she remembered the long gleaming procession of the Three Men, more and more she longed for the Child whom she sought.

In the house, out of the house, up the road, down the street, in castle, in hovel, in farmhouse, in hostelry, in stable went the old woman, swift and silent. When the children saw her they wrinkled up their noses. Something smelled so sweet! The toys she gave them they liked best of all; they kept them for their children and their children's children.

On and on, forever and forever, Babushka searches. A sound on the stairs, a laugh from the babe, a gift on the hearth. "Ah," sing the children, in joy, "Babushka is hunting for the King, hunting, hunting. But see the toys she left us."

In every home in Russia at Christmas time, when there are pretty gifts for boys and girls it is Babushka who is the giver. Babushka, who is searching, searching, searching.

THE ROAD TO BETHLEHEM

The Savior must have been
A docile Gentleman
To come so far, so cold a day
For little fellowmen.

The road to Bethlehem
Since He and I were boys
Was leveled, but for that 'twould be
A rugged billion miles.

Emily Dickenson

CHRISTMAS MORNING

If Bethlehem were here today,
Or this were very long ago,
There wouldn't be a winter time
Nor any cold or snow.

I'd run out through the garden gate,
And down along the pasture walk;
And off beside the cattle barns
I'd hear a kind of gentle talk.

I'd move the heavy iron chain
And pull away the wooden pin;
I'd push the door a little bit
And tiptoe very softly in.

The pigeons and the yellow hens
And all the cows would stand away;
Their eyes would open wide to see
A lady in the manger hay,

If this were very long ago
And Bethlehem were here today.

And Mother held my hand and smiled—
I mean the lady would—and she
Would take the woolly blankets off
Her little boy so I could see.

His shut-up eyes would be asleep,
And he would look like our John,
And he would be all crumpled too,
And have a pinkish color on.

I'd watch his breath go in and out.
His little clothes would all be white.
I'd slip my finger in his hand
To feel how he could hold it tight.

And she would smile and say, "Take care,"
The mother, Mary, would, "Take care";
And I would kiss his little hand
And touch his hair.

While Mary put the blankets back
The gentle talk would soon begin.
And when I'd tiptoe softly out
I'd meet the wise men going in.

Elizabeth Madox Roberts

THE NATIVITY STORY

And it came to pass in those days, that there went out a decree from Caesar Augustus, that all the world should be taxed. And this taxing was first made when Cyrenius was governor of Syria. And all went to be taxed, every one into his own city.

And Joseph also went up from Galilee, out of the city of Nazareth, into Judaea, unto the city of David, which is called Bethlehem, because he was of the house and lineage of David: to be taxed with Mary his espoused wife, being great with child. And so it was, that, while they were there, the days were accomplished that she would be delivered. And she brought forth her firstborn son, and wrapped him in swaddling clothes, and laid him in a manger; because there was no room for them in the inn.

And there were in the same country shepherds abiding in the field, keeping watch over their flock by night. And, lo, the angel of the Lord came upon them, and the glory of the Lord shone round about them; and they were sore afraid. And the angel said unto them, Fear not: for, behold, I bring you good tidings of great joy, which shall be to all people. For unto you is born this day, in the city of David, a Saviour, which is Christ the Lord. And this shall be a sign unto you: Ye shall find the babe wrapped in swaddling clothes, lying in a manger.

And suddenly there was with the angel a multitude of the heavenly host, praising God, and saying, Glory to God in the highest, and on earth peace, good will toward men.

And it came to pass, as the angels were gone away from them into heaven, the shepherds said one to another, Let us now go even unto Bethlehem, and see this thing which is come to pass, which the Lord hath made known unto us.

And they came with haste, and found Mary, and Joseph, and the babe lying in a manger. And when they had seen it, they made known abroad the saying which was told them concerning this child. And all they that heard it wondered at those things which were told them by the shepherds. But Mary kept all these things, and pondered them in her heart. And the shepherds returned, glorifying and praising God for all the things that they had heard and seen, as it was told unto them.

The Gospel according to St. Luke

THE MAGI

Now when Jesus was born in Bethlehem of Judaea in the days of Herod the king, behold, there came wise men from the east to Jerusalem, saying, "Where is he that is born King of the Jews? for we have seen his star in the east, and are come to worship him.

When Herod the king had heard these things, he was troubled, and all Jerusalem with him. And when he had gathered all the chief priests and scribes of the people together, he demanded of them where Christ should be born. And they said unto him, In Bethlehem of Judaea: for thus it is written by the prophet:

And thou Bethlehem, in the land of Juda,

Art not the least among the princes of Juda:

For out of thee shall come a Governor,

That shall rule my people Israel.

Then Herod, when he had privily called the wise men, inquired of them diligently what time the star appeared. And he sent them to Bethlehem, and said, Go and search diligently for the young child; and when you have found him, bring me word again, that I may come and worship him also.

When they had heard the king, they departed; and, lo, the star, which they saw in the east, went before them, till it came and stood over where the young child was. When they saw the star, they rejoiced with exceeding great joy. And when they were come into the house, they saw the young child with Mary his mother, and fell down, and worshipped him: and when they had opened their treasures, they presented unto him gifts; gold, and franincense, and myrrh. And being warned by God in a dream that they should not return to Herod, they departed into their own country another way.

The Gospel according to St. Matthew

For unto us a child is born, unto us a son is given, and the government shall be upon his shoulder; and his name shall be called Wonderful, Counsellor, The mighty God, The everlasting Savior, The Prince of Peace.

Isaiah

ABOUT THE ARTIST:

Natasha Simkhovitch is the pseudonym of Marie S. Stern. Born in 1909, in New York City to Russian immigrant parents she received early instruction in painting from a paternal uncle in the Simkhovitch family. She was awarded a scholarship to the Pratt Institute and began her career as an artist during the Depression. Finding success in the field of children's literature, she has over twenty-five titles to her credit as well as numerous critical citations for her work. Ms. Stern's version of the *Three Little Kittens,* for example, under the signature "Masha," has sold millions of copies and remains in print today.

As a child Ms. Stern loved to draw. "I have been an artist since I was five years old," she recalled, "when I decided I *would be one.*" In more recent years she has taught fine art and sculpture and today lives in Sarasota, Florida, still creating and living with art.

NATASHA SIMKHOVITCH

ACKNOWLEDGEMENTS:

Art: All illustrations originally appeared in *Merry Christmas!* © 1943, Artists and Writers Guild, renewed 1971 by Marie S. Stern. Used with permission of artist.
"The Christmas Cuckoo" adapted from the original in *Granny's Wonderful Chair* (1857) by Frances Browne, as found in *Good Stories for Great Holidays,* © 1913.
"The Small One of Bethlehem" adapted from *Small One, A Story for Those Who Like Christmas and Small Donkeys* by Charles Tazewell, © 1944, Charles Tazewell.
"Babushka" and "Christmas Through a Knothole" by Katharine Gibson, © 1943, Katharine Gibson.
"Cratchits Christmas Dinner" by Charles Dickens, from *A Christmas Carol.*
"A Miserable Merry Christmas" by Lincoln Steffens, excerpt from *The Autobiography of Lincoln Steffens,* Vol. 1, © 1931, by Harcourt Brace and Co., renewed 1959 by Peter Steffens, reprinted by permission of the publisher.
"The Boy Who Laughed at Santa Claus" © 1937, Ogden Nash. Copyright renewed 1965. By permission of Little, Brown, and Company.
"How Come Santa Claus and Christmas and All" by Roark Bradford, excerpt from *How Come Christmas* © 1930, Harper and Row, also published in *Christmas Gif', An Anthology of Christmas Poems, Songs, and Stories, Written By and About African Americans,* Charlesmae Hill Rollins, ed., 1963, 1993.
"The Wooden Shoes of Little Wolff" by François Coppée, adapted from the original found in *Good Stories for Great Holidays,* © 1913.
"Shepherd's Song at Christmas" from the *Langston Hughes Reader,* reprinted with permission of Harold Ober Associates, Inc., © 1958, by Langston Hughes, copyright renewed 1986 by George Huston Bass.
"Keeping Christmas with Mark Twain" from *A Lifetime with Mark Twain: The Memories of Katy Leary* by Mary Lawton; *My Father, Mark Twain* by Clara Clemens; *The Autobiography of Mark Twain.*
"Christmas Morning" from *Under the Tree* by Elizabeth Madox Roberts © 1922, B. W. Huebsch, Inc., renewed 1950 by Ivor S. Roberts, © 1930 by Viking Penguin, Inc., renewed 1958 by Ivor S. Roberts. Used by permission of Viking Penguin, a division of Penguin books USA, Inc.
Considerable effort has been made to trace ownership of texts included in this anthology. Any inadvertent errors or omissions will be corrected in subsequent editions if the publisher is notified.